1

Dear Readers,

This book is not so much about horses, but rather about a complicated relationship. I hope you enjoy Mandy's journey in working it through.

Mandy's Summer

By Savannah Wiebe

ISBN 978-1-6671-9129-4

Mandy's Summer

Chapter 1

BEEP! BEEP! BEEP!

I groaned and rolled over in bed. *Morning couldn't be here already!* I tried to get the annoying beep of my alarm clock out of my head but I knew I had a hungry pony waiting for me outside. I slapped my alarm off and threw off my covers. I stepped over piles of clothes as I made my way to the dresser. I pulled out a white T-shirt and my favorite pair of jeans. I glanced out the window as I pulled my clothes on. A light drizzle was falling which surprised me since it was summer. I groaned. *Just what I need on a Monday morning!* I thought as I pulled out my favorite scarlet red hoodie.

I headed upstairs and saw Mom making coffee in the kitchen.

"Hey honey," Mom said with a sincere smile. "Do you want breakfast before you feed that pony of yours?"

"I'll wait 'til after, but thanks."

I hurried to my sneakers, pulled them on and trudged out into the rain. On the way to the pasture I saw my brothers, James and Dave, working on a quad, and Dad working on his pickup truck which broke down last week. I arrived at the animal pen which was actually part of the bigger pasture. Dad had separated a smaller section to accommodate shelters for the animals so they would be protected in any kind of weather. I reached the wooden fence, and whistled. Immediately Gracey trotted out of her shelter and came to me.

"Hey there, Gracey," I said, scratching behind her ears which was her favorite spot. She nickered and nudged my arm. "Ok, ok, time for breakfast!" I laughed. I grabbed a pitch fork and filled her trough with hay. She nickered happily and began to munch. Our two Jersey steers, King and Timothy, mooed impatiently for their food. "Ok, ok, you too!" I said and forked them their hay. They walked over eagerly. For the next few minutes I made sure they had water, good bedding, and that nothing was wrong or out of shape. "Well, I'll see you later," I said giving Gracey one last rub, and then headed into the house.

I had gotten Gracey from a good neighbour who said she didn't want her anymore. I had been hoping for a horse or pony for years. She was a Chincoteague pony, which was pretty surprising, since there aren't many Chincoteague ponies in Alberta. In fact, I'm not sure if there are any, besides Gracey. She is the best pony I could ever have, and I wouldn't trade her for a million bucks.

I stepped into the house, relieved to be out of the wet weather. My family was already at the table. I kicked off my sneakers and sat down.

"How's that pony of yours, Amanda?" Mom asked as she handed me a plate of pancakes. I smiled. Mom was the only one who called me Amanda; everyone else referred to me as Mandy. I don't mind either name.

"Good," I said, through a mouthful of food. "I think she is fit for the horse show!" I was participating in a horse show in a week and I couldn't wait! Gracey and I had been practicing our low built jumps, and she enjoyed it. But we weren't allowed to ride in the rain. Mom worried that we might slip and fall.

"Oh, and by the way," Mom said, turning towards the kitchen. "Aunt Lucy, Uncle Pete and Violet are arriving from Ottawa today."

I stopped short with a forkful of pancake halfway into my mouth. I dropped my fork and my mouth remained wide open. "No way!" I exclaimed. Violet was one year older than me and she was always complaining if her nails were chipped, or if her hair was out of place. Not only was she always complaining but she was also pretty. Her curly chocolate brown hair was down to her waist, and she had "almost purple" eyes. She could be a model in Paris, or something. "Does she have to come?" I muttered.

Mom gave me a frown. "Of course," she said. "If you were in Violet's place, you wouldn't want to be left out, would you?" I shook my head. Mom didn't understand what Violet was like. When the adults were around, she acted all sweet like we were best friends. But the moment our parents were not in the room, she would start tormenting me. The last time I had seen Violet was when we lived in the city. What would she think of us 'farmers'? Also, she hated horses. What a week this was going to be!

I finished my breakfast with no appetite and excused myself from the table. I wanted to see Gracey. When I arrived at her pen, she had finished her breakfast and was trotting around the pasture. I whistled and she came cantering. "Hey, girl," I said with a smile, as she whinnied. "It turns out that Violet's coming to stay for a week," I said, with an annoyed sigh. "So I want you to be a good girl while she is here, ok?" Gracey bobbed her head in response. I smiled. "Well, I got to go 'coz Mom says I have to prepare the room for my visitor," I said, with a roll of my eyes. I gave her one last pat and headed towards the house.

When I came inside, everyone was at their own thing: James and Dave were playing a board game, Dad had gone out to work on the pickup, and Mom was cleaning the house. But it was my room that Mom was worried about, so I went downstairs to tackle it. The extra mattress was already there leaning against the wall – Dad must have hauled it in with the boys.

My room was a MESS -- it was as if a tornado had blown through there. Clothes where all over the place and my quilts and sheets were tangled up in a lump. And books, magazines, and all sorts of stuff lay all over the place. "I can't believe she has to sleep in *my* room!" I muttered. Mom had mentioned it earlier, and when I heard that, I felt like I was about to explode with fury. But there were only four bedrooms in the house – my parents' room, my brothers' room, my room and a guest room for Uncle Pete and Aunt

Lucy, plus two small offices for my parents. The boys said they didn't want to share their room with a girl, like as if. And Mom or Dad didn't want anybody in their offices, so Mom made me share my room. "I better get to work," I said to myself. As I began picking up my stuff I groaned, "Oh boy, this is going to be a long day."

An hour and a half later, my room was spotless. Everything was organized. And to my surprise, I actually kind of liked it. I set up the mattress, and grabbing the spare pillows, sheets and extra blankets, I made up the bed for Violet. "There," I muttered, "Spotless." I looked at my watch; it was only ten a.m. I still had another eight hours of time to myself!

I left my room and headed outside. I wanted to spend as much time with Gracey as possible because I knew Mom would insist I spend time with Violet. "Hey girl," I said as soon as I reached the pen. My buckskin pony trotted over to me, and nickered. I loved how her black mane and tail contrasted with her buckskin coloring. "Mom expects me to spend time with Violet," I said with a groan. "So I am going to spend as much time as I can with you today." Gracey seemed to understand and bobbed her head. "Good girl," I said. I glanced at the sky. The drizzle had stopped, the sun was starting to peek out from behind a cloud, and the grass was starting to dry. "How would you like a ride today, girl?" Gracey nodded again. I smiled. At least I will have one good thing happen today.

After my hour and a half ride, I groomed Gracey until she was as clean as a brand new dime. Then I worked with her on some tricks I had been teaching her. After that I helped Mom clean the house. While I was vacuuming (although the floor looked fine to me), I heard a shout from the living room. "Here they come!" Mom said excitedly. I looked out the window and saw an SUV roll into the yard. "Here comes the moment," I muttered. I put the vacuum away and headed outside.

My family was standing there. The SUV stopped, and the car doors opened. Aunt

Lucy and Uncle Pete stepped out of the front seats. "Mary!" Aunt Lucy said to Mom (Mom is Aunt Lucy's sister). For the next few minutes everyone was hugging each other. And finally I was the one getting all the attention. "Why, Mandy!" Aunt Lucy said with a delighted gasp. "I declare! You've grown into a young lady – not a little girl anymore! You must have grown 4 inches since last summer." She invited me into a warm bear hug.

"It's good to see you, Aunt Lucy."

"Oh!" Aunt Lucy said. "Violet! Could you come out of the car please?" I heard some shuffling, and the door opened. There was Violet. She was a lot taller than when I last had seen her, and she was still just as pretty. Her dark hair was brought back into a ponytail. She had bracelets, earrings, and necklaces, a burgundy-colored, fashionable jacket and skinny jeans – all which made me uncomfortable, compared to what I was wearing.

"Oh, hello Violet!" Mom said with a hug. "Why, how you've grown! Amanda, take Violet inside and help her get settled in." I held out my hand and said "Hi."

"Hello," Violet replied with a sweet smile and shook my hand. She looked happy, but I could see an icy glare in her eyes which told me she wasn't happy to be here.

I grabbed her two duffle bags but almost dropped them. I was sure there was a thousand tons of clothes in there! "What do you have in here anyway?" I muttered after our parents were out of earshot.

She snorted and rolled her eyes. "None of your business!" she snapped. I rolled my eyes while she wasn't looking. Then I lead the way downstairs. We entered my room and she stared at it for a few seconds before turning to me. "Great room," she grumbled. "Where's my room?"

"Oh, about that," I said. "Well, you are going to have to sleep in my room cause--"

"What!? I have to sleep in your room!"

"Well, the boys don't want to share a room with you, and there's no more rooms unless you want to stay in the barn?"

"I wish my parents would've let me stay home by myself. I mean, I'm stuck here with you!" she lamented.

"Well, here is where you're sleeping, like it or not," I said, gesturing to the mattress on the floor.

"Great," she mumbled. She threw herself onto the mattress and pulled out a jar of nail polish. I stormed out of the room and headed upstairs. Mom was talking with Aunt Lucy while setting the table, asking about the trip, while Dad and Uncle Pete were sitting on the couch with a cup of coffee, deep into conversation about business. For a second, I felt tempted to tell Mom exactly what was going on between Violet and me. But, I think talking would only make things worse. Mom would say to get used to her, or try to be her friend. But I needed to get away from Violet. I went back downstairs to my room to grab one of my favorite novels, *Misty of Chincoteague.* It was especially my favorite since I had a Chincoteague pony of my own. I glared at Violet and then went back upstairs.

After having a turkey dinner, everyone sat down on the couches to watch a movie. Violet came upstairs to join us. We acted like we were best friends, talking and laughing together. But, when the adults weren't looking, we glared at each other. After the movie we got changed and went to bed. Within a few minutes, Violet was sleeping, breathing softly on her pillow. But I couldn't get to sleep. Violet was going to bother me all week, and I didn't want to talk to Mom or Dad about it. I huddled under the covers and gradually began to drift off to sleep. *This is going to be the longest week ever!*

Chapter 2

I didn't let my alarm beep away. I slapped it almost the second it started. I glanced at Violet, who sat up in bed with a jolt and glared at me with her sleepy eyes. "Did you set that alarm on purpose, just to wake me up?" she asked.

"No!" I huffed out. "I've got a pony to feed."

"Whatever!" Violet grumbled and threw the covers over her head. I sighed.

I grabbed my clothes and went to get changed in the bathroom. When I was about to open the door to go outside, I heard a voice stop me.

"Amanda," Mom said as she held a dish towel.

I turned. "Yeah?"

"How is everything going with you and Violet?"

I almost burst out with my feelings, but I held back. "Fine," I said with a reassuring smile.

"I'm glad to hear that." I felt bad lying to Mom but I wasn't sure if Violet would ever change her attitude, so I didn't know if it would help to tell her.

When I closed the door behind me, the air was already hot. I hadn't enjoyed the drizzle yesterday, but a hot day was even worse. I hurried towards Gracey's pen, and I didn't even have to whistle this time. She came trotting up to me the moment I reached the fence. "Hey, girl," I said with a smile. My mood was starting to change. "Violet is being worse than ever," I said. "But maybe she might change when we get to know each other better." I couldn't believe I just said that! But maybe it would come true. After feeding Gracey and King and Timothy, I asked, "Would you like to go riding today, girl?" She seemed to nod her head in agreement. "Ok," I said, as I hoisted myself over the fence. I didn't even need a saddle or helmet to ride her because Gracey was so reliable. Even if I were to gallop with no hands, I probably wouldn't fall off. But just as I was hoisting myself onto her back, I saw Mom running up to me.

"Honey, there will be no riding today," she said. "I want you to spend time with Violet."

"But Mom--!"

But Mom was already quickly walking back to the house.

I sighed. Gracey needed exercise and besides, I had to practice for a show. "Sorry girl," I said as I slipped off her back. "No riding today." I started to walk away, but Gracey whinnied in protest. "I know! I know!" I said with a laugh. "I'm going to have to ride you tomorrow." I gave her one last rub and hurried off to the house.

When I entered the front door, the pleasant smell of bacon and eggs greeted me. I could see Violet talking with Dad, but when she saw me, she glared. I glared back.

After breakfast I put my dishes in the sink. Just as I was about to go to my room Mom asked me, "Would you want to show Violet your pony?" I hesitated. I didn't want Violet to call Gracey a nag, or anything like that, but I just nodded. Violet put her dishes in the sink and smiled at Mom, but glared at me.

When we got outside, we headed for the pen. I whistled. Gracey came to us and I smiled. I turned to look at Violet. She was keeping her distance and had a nervous look on her face. "Don't you like horses?" I asked, although I already knew the answer.

"No!" she snapped. "They smell, and I don't want to ruin my clothes."

I rolled my eyes, "It's totally safe. Gracey is really sweet." Violet shrugged, and walked slowly towards the fence. Gracey seemed to notice she was nervous, and began to walk away. "Hey, it's ok, girl," I said soothingly.

Violet came closer and was about to pet her when Gracey began to sneeze. "Watch out!" I shouted, "She's about to--" But it was too late! Gracey sneezed and it landed all over Violet's shirt. She shrieked and jumped backwards, her foot landing in a manure pile.

"How could you!" she shrieked. "You did this on purpose, didn't you?"

"No!" I snapped. "I told you to get out of the way, but--"

"Argh!" she said with disgust and stormed off to the house.

When I heard the door slam, I burst out laughing, nearly falling to the ground. Gracey stared at me uneasily. "Sorry, girl," I said,
"but it's just too funny!" And then I burst out laughing again.

After that, I went back inside and went to the boys' room. They were better to be with right now. "Hey, sis," Dave said without looking up from their board game.

"Hey," I said. I sighed and flopped onto James' bed. "She's driving me nuts!" I exclaimed, making my brothers jump.

"Who?" James asked.

"Violet! She's always so whiny! She doesn't like horses! I don't get why she's even here! If she thinks we are--"

I heard someone clear their throat. I turned around and there was Violet! I gulped, feeling a bit guilty about what I had just said. "Violet," I started, "I'm sorry. I didn't know you were standing there..."

Violet stood at the door with her hands on her hips, her eyes ablaze. "You know *what?*" she lashed out. "I don't *want* to be here! And *I don't like you!*"

"Well, *I don't like you either!*" I snapped back.

"*Fine!*" she said, and stormed off to my room, slamming the door behind her.

Dave and James looked at me with surprise. "Wow!" Dave said slowly, "I knew you guys don't get along, but I didn't know it was *that* bad!"

"I know!" I said. "What do I do about it? I don't want to be her archenemy forever!"

"Well, maybe you should treat her like a friend?" James suggested.

"Maybe," I said. "But I don't think that will work. I mean she's pretty snappy right now, and she doesn't care *one hoot* for our farm lifestyle."

"Well, that's all I have to say," James said. "Maybe you should just try it."

I sighed, and nodded. "Maybe. Thanks for the advice, guys."

"No problem," Dave said with a smile. I smiled back. This was one of those moments that I really appreciated having my brothers around. I didn't want to tell Mom and Dad because I thought they wouldn't understand. Even though my brothers could be really rough and annoying, they were still my brothers.

I headed off to my room hoping that what my brothers suggested would work. I opened my door and saw Violet looking at a fashion magazine. "Hi," I said flatly. She didn't respond. "Look," I started. "I'm sorry for saying those things, and I'm hoping we can be friends."

She looked up from her magazine, her eyes icy. "You're kidding right? Be friends with *you?*"

"Well, yeah."

"I don't want to be here, and we don't like each other, so what's the point?" she said, returning her gaze to her magazine.

I felt anger rise in me. This wasn't going to work! "You know what? You're right! I don't get how this is going to work, either!" I stormed off towards the stairs. What was the point of trying to be her friend? She was annoying, snobby, and she didn't even like me! But in spite of this, my mind kept telling me to keep trying, so that was what I was going to do.

Chapter 3

The next day was even hotter than yesterday.
Dad said we were going swimming and to my
surprise, Violet looked like she was going to
enjoy it. We got changed, packed, and got
into the van. Mom wanted Violet and I to sit
together. I told her we had a swimming pool
nearby and she replied saying she was glad we
had some actual "civilization" around here. I
almost laughed when I heard that. Maybe
she wasn't so bad after all. We finally arrived
at the 'swimming pool' which was actually a
canal -- and we didn't have to pay a cent to
use it!

We stepped out of the car and Violet frowned, "I don't see any swimming pool?"

I giggled, "You're staring right at it, silly! It's right there." I stepped closer towards to the canal. The cool, swift-moving water made me want to jump right in to get away from the sticky, hot day.

"No way am I going in that canal thing!" she exclaimed. I frowned. My hopeful thoughts about Violet were fading away.

I shrugged and went onto the car bridge. We used it to jump from -- sort of like a diving board. As I stepped onto the edge and prepared to jump, I heard Violet call out, "Are you sure you want to go in there?" I was surprised, I didn't think she would care if I was dragged by a shark into the depths of the sea.

"Yep," I said confidently.

"But I've heard some kids have drowned in these things!" she said with concern. That was true. Some kids had drowned in canals but they probably didn't have the right supervision, or they didn't know how to swim. And I was a strong swimmer because of my years of practice. I just shrugged and dived into the water. The cold water closed over my head making me feel less grumpy. Instead of surfacing I kept my head under the water to trick Violet. Before I was visible I heard a terrified scream and then I resurfaced.

"I'm fine!" I said with a small laugh.

Violet looked surprised at first but then a light pink blush covered her cheeks. *"I knew that!"* she retorted, trying to cover up her embarrassment. I knew she didn't.

"C'mon!" I said. "It's fun!" Violet shook her head, but I kept urging her. "Are you scared?" I asked with a grin.

"No!" she snapped as a deeper color of red flushed her cheeks.

"Then, c'mon!"

"Fine!" she snapped. She stepped over the railing and jumped.

"See? It's--" I started to say.

"AHHHH!" I heard a piercing scream. I whipped around. Was Violet drowning? But I didn't see her drowning. She was pointing at something. "There's a dead fish in here!" she shrieked. I saw the dead fish and sighed as I rolled my eyes.

"You were freaking out? Over a dead FISH??" I yelled. "I thought you were drowning!"

"Whatever, Mandy!" she yelled back. "I'm not swimming in here!" She waded to the edge and climbed out of the canal. She grabbed her towel and sat in the car. I sighed. *Did she have to make such a big deal over a fish?* I climbed up to the bridge where Dad and the boys were about to jump.

"So, it isn't working that well, huh?" Dave asked.

"Nope," I said flatly. "I just don't get her."

"Well, let's forget about her for now," Dave said, "Let's just enjoy the day."

And we did. We spent our time jumping and diving off the bridge, practicing flips, and all sorts of stuff. Aunt Lucy persuaded Violet to come out again, but she only stuck her feet in the water. After about half an hour of diving and jumping, Dad pumped up a large floaty and we floated down the canal. Violet joined us. I spent most of my time relaxing, sticking my fingers in the water. I talked a bit with Aunt Lucy about Ottawa and stuff. I was wondering if Aunt Lucy could help me with Violet because she was her mom so she knew her best. But it was not a good time, Violet being right there. And I wasn't sure if it was a good idea anyway, even to talk about it later, so I decided to keep my mouth shut.

After swimming, I asked Mom if I could ride Gracey and practice for the show, since we didn't go riding yesterday. At first Mom wanted me to spend more time with Violet. I told her I had spent much more time with Violet than riding. I could spend more time with her later (although I wasn't looking forward to it). Finally, she agreed.

I went to a small storage trailer where all my tack, feed, and all sorts of other things were. I grabbed my grooming box and tack, and headed over to Gracey's pen. She came rushing over to me and nickered. I smiled. "Hey, girl! I can ride you today since I didn't get to yesterday. Would you like that, girl?" Gracey nodded her head, and I smiled. "Good girl! Now, let's get all that dust off you! You're a mess!" I began brushing her with the curry comb, then the hard bristle brush, and finally the soft bristle brush. I swept it over her coat making her look like a show pony. Then I brushed all the knots out of her mane and tail. Finally with a hoof pick I removed the muck out of her feet. I didn't want her to fall while we were practicing. After her grooming, I smoothed the saddle pad onto her back. Then I took the saddle and placed it on top of the pad. Grabbing the girth, I tightened it, and pulled down the stirrup irons. After that, I put on the bridle. Finally I pulled on my helmet which I had received for Christmas last year.

"C'mon, girl," I said, tugging on the reins.
"Let's ride!" I had set up my jumping course
in the yard rather than the pasture because
that's where we kept the steers. I led her to
the yard and hopped into the saddle. I spent
the next few minutes walking, trotting, and
cantering. Gracey had to stretch her legs.
After that I aimed her for the first jump: a
vertical, about three feet high. I cantered
towards it and Gracey jumped it easily.
"Good girl!" I said soothingly and patted her
neck. The next jump was a parallel oxer. I felt
nervous as I neared the jump. She jumped it,
but a stride too early. The front pole
thundered to the ground. I sighed. I needed
to work on that one -- but I wasn't going to
focus on that right now. I aimed Gracey
towards the next jump with three poles.
Unfortunately, those types of jumps are hard
to judge. I didn't speed her up fast enough.
She hesitated in front of the jump, but
jumped it. The top pole fell. The rest of the
course went well with Gracey only making
one refusal on another vertical. I turned her
around to redo the course and hoped to do
better.

An hour and a half later I turned Gracey out to pasture. She cantered away happily. I sighed contentedly feeling pretty good about the show. After the first round of jumping, the rest went much better. By the last round, we only knocked down one pole. I think we *just might* get a ribbon at the show. I watched Gracey for a few minutes before heading towards the house.

Now, to spend time with Violet. I wasn't looking forward to it but there was no way to avoid it. Once in the house, I kicked off my tall riding boots and headed down stairs. Violet was looking at magazines which covered every inch of the floor in my room!

"What are you doing?" I barked at her.

She jumped and glared at me. "Looking at fashion magazines, what else would I be doing?" she said, turning back to the page.

"This is *my* room!" I said, maybe a little too loudly. I kicked a magazine towards her.

"Hey!" she shouted as she snatched the magazine and put it under her pillow. "This is *my* stuff!"

"If you don't like me, why didn't you just stay home?" I snapped at her.

She let out a loud, disgusted sigh. "It was my parents' dumb idea! If it wasn't for that, I would be cruising at home right now!"

"Why don't you just ask you parents to take you home? I mean, if you don't like me or like being here!" I snarled.

"Fine! Maybe I will!" she screamed back. She stormed upstairs. I wish I would've kept my mouth shut. Now Mom and Dad would want to know what's going on. And that would make me nervous. I went to the boys' room. Maybe, just maybe, they could help me. I entered their room, explaining what just had happened.

"Well, I don't know," James said. "Maybe she'll come around eventually. She hasn't been here long enough to really get to know us."

"Maybe," I said with a sigh. "I'm just not sure I can take her any longer sleeping in my room."

"You could talk to Mom about it," James suggested. "She could probably handle your problem."

"No way!" I exclaimed. "I'm not sure I want her to get involved. I mean, I'm twelve years old! I can handle my own problems!"

"Well, it doesn't look like it, from the way you're sounding, does it?" Dave said, and they snickered.

I rolled my eyes. "Very funny!" I said, and stuck out my tongue.

"Here's another option," James said. "You could talk to God about it." I hadn't thought of that.

"I'll try that," I said. "Thanks guys."

I walked out of the room feeling a little more relaxed. Maybe that's what I needed to do. Talk to God about it. I decided not to think about Violet right now. I could smell dinner from here so I headed up stairs to help with supper.

Chapter 4

Over the next few days, Violet grew worse
and worse, and I grew more and more
grumpy. I was especially mad when Aunt
Lucy said she was enjoying it here so much
that she decided they should stay another
week if my parents were okay with it, which
they were. I wasn't sure if I could take Violet
any longer. I had talked to God about it, but
he hadn't responded yet. Finally, I couldn't
take it anymore. I needed to talk to Mom. I
walked into the kitchen where she was
washing dishes and humming. When she
noticed me, she smiled.

"Hey, honey," she said.

"Hey, Mom," I took a deep breath. "Mom, I need to talk to you about something."

"What is it, Amanda?"

I took another deep breath. "It's about Violet," I started, "I just can't take her anymore and--"

"I know," Mom said with a smile.

"You...do?" I said, surprised. "But I thought-"

"Lucy and I wanted you two to get to know each other better. That's what part of this trip was about."

"What do I do about her?" I asked. "She isn't trying to be friendly at all."

"Maybe that's because you're not being nice to her." I felt guilty when she said that, but I hadn't thought about that before. And it was true -- I hadn't been very nice, either.

"What if she keeps acting the way she does?"

"Just continue to be nice to her," she said. "She'll come around eventually." I thought about it -- it just might work and it might make us both less miserable.

"Thanks, Mom," I said, wrapping my arms around her in a hug.

"You're welcome, sweetheart. Go talk to Violet now." I nodded and headed for the stairs and then turned back.

"Mom?"

"Yeah?"

"I have a confession to make."

"What's that?"

"I lied . . . when you asked if everything was going ok with Violet and me."

"Well, you're forgiven."

"Thanks, Mom," I gave her one more hug and headed down stairs . . .

. . . perhaps this was the answer to my prayer.

I entered my room. Violet was painting her nails. She looked up and glared at me when I came in. I stood there for a moment looking at her, trying to think of what to say.

Violet shifted uncomfortably when she saw my gaze on her. "What do you want?" she demanded, "Have you come to dump my bag and steal my nail polish?"

"No," I said. I sighed. "Violet, look," I started, "I was wondering if we could be...well...ah...friends? I'm tired of fighting with you. It would be better for both of us."

She stared at me. Her face seemed to soften a little and her "almost purple" eyes seemed warmer for a second. When she opened her mouth I thought she was going to say "yes", but instead she gave a flat, "No".

I sighed, not wanting to draw this out any longer. I shrugged. "Just think about it, ok?" I left the room. I wasn't sure if what I said had done any good, but the look in her eyes seemed to indicate a slight flicker of wanting to be friends. Maybe she was too afraid to admit it. *We'll just have to wait and see.* And then I walked away, wanting to get a ride on Gracey before dinner.

Chapter 5

My alarm beeped and I slapped it off quickly. I looked at the time -- it was five-thirty a.m. and it was Saturday -- time for the riding show! Over the past few days I had been practicing pretty hard and I thought Gracey and I were ready. I threw back my covers and tip-toed over to my dresser because I didn't want to wake Violet up! I had a quick shower and got changed into my skinny jeans and T-shirt. I slipped on my sneakers and headed outside. It was still pretty dark but dawn was beginning to break over the horizon with red and pink splashes through the clouds. I hurried towards Gracey's pen.

"Hey, girl!" I said. Gracey trotted up to me. "We are having a show today -- are you ready to win some ribbons, girl?" Even in the dim light I could see her bob her head. I smiled. While she ate her breakfast I got everything ready: my saddle, first aid, my show clothes, and an assortment of other things I needed for the day. I loaded these into the back of our SUV. I double-checked that everything was there, and was in order, and then headed inside. Mom had cooked up a special breakfast of pancakes, eggs, bacon and sausage for me. My mouth watered when I saw the food.

"Why the special meal?" I asked with a grin.

"You need your energy," Mom said.

"Thanks Mom!" I gave her a big hug and began eating the delicious food.

After that, I checked everything one more time. Then I went to get Gracey. I haltered her and she didn't mind me leading her into the trailer. I was afraid she might bolt or spook because she had rarely been in one, but she handled it like a pro, and went in easily. I hung up her hay net and Gracey began munching immediately. I hopped into the truck. Dad started the engine and we headed off to the horse show grounds. Mom said she would follow later in our other truck and Violet and her family would come in their SUV after breakfast. I felt excitement bubble up inside me. *I think I just might get a ribbon in this riding show!*

Almost an hour later we reached our destination. Other riders, horses, and trailers covered the grounds. I looked at my watch. It was almost seven thirty -- I only had an hour to get ready! I hurried to the checkup tent to register and get my show number which I would tie around my waist. After getting registered, I got changed into my show clothes: breeches, tall riding boots, a white blouse, and a black riding jacket. And then I began to get Gracey ready. I didn't have time to do anything fancy to her mane or tail, so I just combed them until they were untangled and fluffy. Then I began grooming her and checked her hooves to make sure there was nothing that could cause Gracey to get hurt.

After that I tacked her up. I put the saddle pad and saddle on her back and then slipped the bridle on her face. I wrapped navy blue polo raps onto her legs to protect them. My turn was still half an hour away but I wanted to make sure I was ready.

"Amanda!" I turned from straightening Gracey's forelock to see Aunt Lucy, Mom, Violet, and Uncle Pete walk up to me. I hugged the adults and just stared at Violet. She looked a lot more comfortable, so I knew she was thinking about what I had said the other day. Aunt Lucy and Mom gave each other a hopeful look, but I didn't want them to jump to any conclusions because I didn't know if Violet had made up her mind yet.

Half an hour later I heard a voice echo across the grounds, "Amanda Peters, come to the jumping ring." I jumped up feeling butterflies in my stomach. *This is it!*

"Go get 'em!" Aunt Lucy encouraged. I smiled at her, and led Gracey towards the jumping arena. It was a large outdoor arena. I gulped at the sight of the jumps which were the same height as the ones we had practiced on, but way more complicated with flower boxes, rails, and other things. *We can do this! We can do this!* I chanted in my head as we entered the arena. But -- I still had nerves. I climbed into the saddle and began to warm up by walking, trotting and cantering. After that I halted Gracey at one end of the arena where the course started. I had to wait for the bell before starting.

The bell rang and I sent Gracey into a canter. The first jump, a high cross rail, was an easy one for Gracey. The next jump, another cross rail, was a breeze for her – she jumped it amazingly. "Good girl," I murmured, patting her on the neck. But the next jump was ahead. I hadn't prepared her for this third jump, a one-railed bar with a flower box underneath. She slid to a stop. I turned her around and aimed her for the jump again. This time she jumped it, but hit the rail which landed on the ground. I didn't want to focus on that one jump so I kept going. I cantered around to the other side of the arena, and began the other half of the course. The next few jumps were different types of double oxers. I aimed Gracey towards the first one. She jumped it easily, and then I headed for the second double oxer. That one also went well, but the next oxer she jumped a second too early, again causing the rail to clunk to the ground. We jumped the next few jumps easily, and then it was the last one. Everything seemed to go into slow motion. Gracey leapt as if it was nothing. I smiled as the crowd cheered. I could see Mom and Dad in the bleachers. I cantered out of the ring and hopped out of the saddle.

"You were amazing, honey!" Mom exclaimed as she gave me a hug.

"Thanks, Mom!" I said with a smile. I knew that hadn't been my best ride, but I was proud of myself and Gracey. "You did amazing," I said as I hugged Gracey's neck. "C'mon. Let's cool you off."

An hour later, I led Gracey back into the riding ring to get my results. The judges had the ribbons ready. "First place goes to Amy Jackson on Checkers," the judge said over the loud speaker. The crowd exploded into applause as Amy went to collect her blue ribbon. "Second place goes to Karlie Spencer on Penny," the announcer said.

Finally, after many riders they announced me. "Ninth place goes to Amanda Peters on Gracey." When I went to receive my 9th place ribbon, I smiled at the judge and then headed back to Gracey. *I could've done better in the show, but it was my first horse show, right? I will get better the more I practice.*

"You did great, honey!" Mom exclaimed as I exited the arena.

"Thanks."

"So, I guess we'll be seeing you at another show this year." Dad said as we walked back to the trailer.

"Maybe."

I looked at Dad who looked surprised. "Maybe?" he echoed.

I sighed. "I am proud of the placing I got.

But...." I stopped for a second. "I didn't work hard enough. I need to practice more. I think I'm going to wait 'til next year before I do another show." I also thought I should drop back to a lower level if I wanted to succeed in show jumping.

"I think you made a wise choice," Mom said with a smile.

"So do I," Dad said. I smiled. I was glad they understood.

After celebrating at a special restaurant we made our way back home. I was about to go inside to relax a little when I heard a voice.

"Mandy! Wait!" I turned to see Violet jogging up to me.

"What is it?" I asked, not really sure what she was going to say. *She's probably going to say something like I did a horrible job on my show.*

She took a deep breath. "I just wanted to say you did a swell job today," she said with her hands in her jeans' pockets.

"Thanks," I said with a tiny smile. She walked off, but then turned and walked up to me again. "Ok, that isn't all I have to say."

"What do you have to say?" I asked her.

"I'm sorry for the way I've been acting. I was just jealous, I guess."

"You? Jealous?" I almost burst out laughing.

"Yeah," she said, embarrassed. "I wanted to be the center of attention. I'm not usually like that."

For a moment I was speechless. I didn't know what to say. Finally, I found the right words. "It's ok," I said, walking closer towards her. "I'm sorry too for being…well, mean."

"You're forgiven," she said. And we burst out laughing.

After dinner Violet and I headed downstairs to watch a movie, just the two of us.

"What do you want to watch?' I asked pulling the DVDs off the shelf.

"What about..." she shuffled through the DVDs, "...The Lord of the Rings?"

"Perfect!" I said. I had watched that movie countless times, but it was one of my favorites. Violet went to get some popcorn. She dumped it in a bowl and we started the movie. When I looked at her she smiled back at me and I suddenly had the feeling this was going to be one of the best summers of my life.

I silently said, "Thanks God, for answering my prayer."

Chapter 6

"I'm still not sure about this," Violet said nervously, as we walked towards Gracey's pen at six in the morning.

"Don't worry," I reassured her. "Gracey is excellent at helping new riders." I had convinced Violet to have a riding lesson. She said the only time she had ridden a horse, was when she had sat on one as a baby. She was still pretty nervous about it, but looked determined.

"But -- what if I fall?" she asked, her eyes filled with fear.

"You won't," I said. "Now let's feed Gracey."
I walked up to the fence and whistled.
Gracey came trotting up to me and I touched
her soft muzzle. Violet stayed back. "It's ok,"
I said. "You can pet her."

"Does she bite?"

"Nope. She is the sweetest pony in the whole
world."

She took a deep breath and began walking
over to her. "Hiyah, girl," she said nervously
when she reached the fence. "I'm Violet." She
slowly held out her hand. Gracey smelled it.

"You can pet her," I said gently. Violet
reached her hand towards Gracey, and gently
began to pet Gracey's muzzle.

"It's so soft!" she exclaimed with a smile.

"Yeah."

For the next five minutes I showed Violet the
types of feed, and how to feed Gracey with

her hand. After that I was ready to teach the lesson. "Ok," I said cheerfully, "Now it's time for your riding lesson."

Violet began to look all nervous again, but she took a deep breath and smiled. "Ok," she said.

I grabbed my grooming kit and tack and went into the pen. We had put the steers in the other pen to keep them from bothering us. I caught Gracey and tied her to the fence. "Ok," I said, taking the curry comb from the grooming kit, "first we use this brush to get all the dirt off and stuff, and you move it in circles like this." I showed her how to massage her back with the brush and then handed it to her. "I want you to try," She moved it along Gracey's back exactly the way I showed her.

She looked at me. "Like this?" she asked as she continued brushing.

"Yes, exactly like that," I said with a nod. We continued the same thing with all the brushes. I did the hoof pick since Violet was still pretty new to this type of thing. Then I showed her how to tack up. After that we were ready for the lesson.

"Here. You need this," I said, tossing her my helmet. She caught it and buckled it under her chin. "Ok, now just swing your leg over and shove your feet into the stirrups." Violet still looked nervous, but she nodded.

"Ok," she said. She swung her leg over but landed awkwardly in the saddle. She fixed herself and shoved her feet into the stirrups while I held Gracey tight.

"Ok. Now I am going to lead you around." I clucked my tongue and Gracey started off at a walk.

"This feels weird," she said, still looking nervous but after a few minutes she seemed to get the hang of it a little more. "Hey, this is fun!" she exclaimed.

"Do you want to try a trot?" I asked. She started to look nervous all over again.

"Am I ready for that?"

"You sure look like it. You're a pro at this already!" What I said seemed to give her confidence. She straightened up and nodded. "C'mon, girl!" I clucked my tongue and Gracey burst into a trot.

"Whoa!" Violet exclaimed, nearly falling out of the saddle. I pulled Gracey to a stop and looked at her with concern.

"You ok?"

"Yeah. It just feels so weird! I think I'm done for today." She took off her helmet and handed it to me

"Are you sure?" I asked.

"Yeah. But it was fun!" she exclaimed. I sighed with relief. I was glad she had enjoyed her ride.

"That was fun!" Violet exclaimed again, as she took off Gracey's tack. "Do you think I could ride again?"

"Really?" I was surprised. I had just suggested a small lesson, not expecting her to take more!

"Yeah," she said, beginning to brush Gracey's back with the curry comb.

"Sure!" I was excited -- it was like I was a riding instructor, owning my own stables. How fun would that be! We continued to brush her in silence. After I turned Gracey loose, we headed towards the house for breakfast.

After breakfast, Dad decided to take us swimming again. It was an especially hot day and a good swim would probably be refreshing. We loaded our stuff and drove to the canal. When we arrived, Violet looked disgusted, "Do you think there's more dead fish in there?" she asked.

I burst out laughing. "Yeah. But you'll get used to it."

"I hope so," she said with a nervous smile on her face. And eventually she did. At first, every time she saw anything gross or disgusting, she would scream and that would make me laugh out loud.

"Hey, this *is* kinda fun! I mean, it's not the same as a swimming pool or a hot tub or anything, but it's still fun!"

"See?" I said. After a while we just sat on floaties and let the current pull us down stream. I smiled. I had a feeling that Violet and I were going to be best friends.

Chapter 7

On Monday Violet and I spent the morning exploring the prairies and stuff. She really seemed to be getting used to farm life. She always came out to help me feed the animals and even shovel manure. The only thing she was still scared of were the chickens because they pecked her feet.

Later in the day, I checked my watch. It was almost three o'clock in the afternoon. I glanced around as I hadn't seen Violet since lunch. I headed downstairs towards my room and stopped when I heard muffled voices from there. I walked quietly towards the door and peeked through the opening. Violet was sitting cross-legged on the floor with her parents' laptop open in front of her. It looked like she was talking to some of her friends from back home. I leaned forward to listen. I knew eavesdropping was rude but I wanted to know what they were saying.

"...it's been pretty fun, actually," Violet said as she painted her nails. "I have had all sorts of fun."

"Like what?..." asked a blonde girl, sarcastically, "...shovelling horse manure?" Her two friends burst out laughing and even though I couldn't see Violet's face, I saw her stiffen and sensed her frowning.

"No..." she said, a bit thrown off. "There are lots of other things to do to, like taking care of the animals and stuff."

"Don't tell me you're turning into one of those silly, country folk, are you?" said the blonde girl, her face also turning into a frown.

I felt anger rise up in my chest. *How could a random, ignorant girl say such things about us?*

"No way!" Violet said emphatically. "I don't want to be here! I hate it here!"

WHAT?! My mind shrieked. I almost said it out loud. I couldn't believe what I was hearing. I thought she liked it here! And now, here she was telling her friends she hates it here?

"I totally want to go home!" Violet exclaimed. "I don't want to be here another second."

"Good," the blonde girl said with a nod. "I got to go. I have to go shopping at the mall. Talk to you later!" After they said good-bye, Violet stepped out of the room and stepped into me.

"Mandy!" she said with surprise, but I could tell she knew I had heard their conversation.

"Do you really think..." I started, "...that we are some silly, country folk!?" I snapped. "NO!" she said, her eyes wide in alarm. "I was just saying that to--"

"If you really think that, then why don't you just go hang out with your friends from the city!" I screamed, maybe a little too loud.

"But I didn't--" she started weakly.

"Whatever!" I snapped and stormed off. I couldn't believe she would think such things about us! *I shouldn't have believed her from the start.* I didn't want to be friends with her anymore! No matter what she would say! *But, maybe you can forgive her,* a tiny voice said. I pushed it out of my mind.

Over the next few days Violet tried to talk to me about it, but I ignored her and came up with excuses to avoid her. I didn't even let her feed the animals with me. After a while, she seemed to give up. She sat gloomily on the couch and sometimes I heard her sniffle. But I still ignored her. *If she was really my friend, why would she say those things about us? Why would she say that she hated it here?* Suddenly the tiny voice popped back into my mind. *Just forgive her,* the voice encouraged, but again I pushed it out of my mind. I was pretty sure our relationship was over.

Chapter 8

I turned over in bed and looked at my alarm clock. It was almost six thirty. I looked at Violet and turned around because I didn't want to see her right now. I got out of bed and changed into jeans and a T-shirt and crept upstairs.

Mom was preparing breakfast. When I entered the kitchen, she smiled at me.

"Good morning. How was your sleep?"

"Fine," I grumbled as I sat down and rested my headed on my arm. Mom raised her eyebrows at me.

"Well, that tone didn't sound like it was fine. What happened?" she asked as she sat down. I sighed. I wish I hadn't said anything but now that it was out, I might as well tell her.

"Well," I started. "Everything with me and Violet is just kinda upside down."

Mom raised her eyebrows at me again. "Well, from the looks of you two, you seemed to be getting along. Did she do something to make you mad?"

"Yes, she told her friends she hated it here and that she wanted to go home."

"Hmmm...yes, that would be upsetting, for sure," Mom said with understanding. "How did you respond to that?"

"Well...I guess I wasn't very nice...I reacted and told her to go home since she hates it here..." I felt my cheeks go pink.

Mom sighed as she stroked my dirty blonde hair. "Oh, honey." We just sat there quietly for a moment.

Then Mom said, "She might have just said it to make her friends back off."

I sighed. I hadn't thought about that. I felt pretty guilty as I had assumed she had done it because she really meant it. Now that I thought about it from that angle, it still was upsetting, but my reaction bothered me. I felt my cheeks go pink again.

"It's going to be ok, honey. God is pretty good at fixing these things if we ask for his help. Why don't we pray?" Mom suggested as she hugged me.

"Yeah," I sighed, ". . . that sounds good."

We bowed our heads and mom started, "Dear Lord, thank you that you are good at fixing things - broken hearts, broken relationships, even broken bodies. Please help Amanda and Violet to work out this tangled situation. We need your help. In Jesus' name."

I continued, "Lord, I'm sorry I haven't been nice to Violet. I know I need to say sorry. Just not sure how. Please help me. Amen."

"Mom, how *do* I say sorry?"

"Just say it normally," she said with a smile. I hugged her.

"Thanks, Mom!" I wrapped my arms around her tighter. She laughed.

"Go tell her now," she said, as I pulled away. "I bet she is awake."

I nodded, and went downstairs. When I opened my door I found Violet sitting on her mattress.

"Hi," I said cautiously. She jumped and stared at me.

"Hi," she said quickly and grabbed her cell phone to cover up her awkwardness in looking at me and talking to me.

"Look," I said. She glanced at me as she was scrolling through her messages. "I'm sorry for the way I've been. I didn't mean to be that way. I guess I just overreacted." I blushed again. She looked back at her phone. "Look,

I'm sorry, ok!?" I snapped. She looked a little startled. I put my hand over my mouth. "I'm sorry," I said more gently. "I didn't mean it to come out that way--"

"It's ok!" she exclaimed and smiled.

I blinked. "Are you sure?" I asked. "Like, really sure?"

"Yep," she said. "I was only saying those things to my friends to make them back off." she blushed.

"Can we be friends again?" I asked her.

She smiled teasingly. "Oh, I don't know...." she said, and for a second I thought she really meant it.

"You mean--" I started.

"I'm just kidding!" she exclaimed, as she saw my face. "We can totally be friends again!" She grabbed me in a hug. "I'm sorry, too. I shouldn't have said what I did to my city friends. I really do like being here – that's the truth! I was intimidated by their comments and wanted to be accepted by them. I can't believe I'm so fickle," she said with a blush.

I grabbed her in another hug. "I forgive you. Now, you want to go and feed that pony of mine with me?" I asked.

She smiled. "Yes, I'd love that!"

I walked out with her and we linked arms. I was so glad that we were friends again!

Chapter 9

As the week passed, it was as if I had never been mad at Violet. We spent a lot of time exploring, going fishing and swimming. And Violet asked again if she could have more riding lessons. I have to admit, she was getting really good! I even led her over a jump yesterday. Now the week was over and Violet was going back to Ottawa. I was sad to see her go but she said we would keep in touch.

"I will write you a letter whenever I can," she said, as they loaded up their stuff.

"I'm going to miss you!" I gave her a hug.

"I'm going to miss you, too!" She wrapped her arms around me. "Maybe I can come back next summer."

Aunt Lucy and Uncle Pete said their last goodbyes and headed into the car. As they were driving away down the road, I waved and I could see Violet waving back. I watched and waved until I couldn't see them anymore.

A week later Mom came into the living room holding a letter. "This is for you," she said, handing it to me. I looked at the envelope. It was from Violet!

"Thanks, Mom!" I gave her a quick hug. I ripped open the envelope and began to read the letter which also came with a picture. It was a pony! I squealed and continued to read.

Dear Mandy,

I miss you so much! But I have some exciting news . . . I bought a Miniature horse! He is so cute! I named him Cinnamon Bun because of his color, and cause he is so sweet. I am also taking riding lessons. I am riding a pony named Jack, and he is also very sweet. Mom and Dad miss you too! And the rest of your family. I hope to see you again soon. But Mom says that it will probably have to be in the summer cause of school. Give a hug from me to Gracey!!!

Sincerely,
    Violet

I smiled and immediately got out a piece of paper and a pen and began to write:

Dear Violet,

I miss you too! And that is AWESOME that you have a Miniature horse! The name is so cute! And that is great that you are taking riding lessons. You should enter a show some time. You were getting really good when you were riding Gracey. Hope your family is doing well. Gracey misses you! She is always looking for you whenever I go to feed her or ride her. I hope to see you again next *summer (or sooner). Good luck with riding lessons. And say hi to your family for me.*

Sincerely,
   Mandy

I folded the paper and put it in an envelope. I would send it the next time we went to the post office. I smiled. Who knew that your archenemy would become your best friend! This was the hardest but best summer I had ever had!

About the Author

Savannah Wiebe lives in Southern Alberta. This is her second published book. She has two sisters and one brother, and is enjoying farm life with them on a small acreage -- and definitely prefers farm life over city life. She helps water the stock and the 30 trees they planted this spring. She and her sisters take horseback riding lessons and dance lessons.